The Oscar J. Noodleman Television Network

BOOKS BY STEPHEN MANES

The Oscar J. Noodleman Television Network:
The Second Strange Thing That Happened to Oscar Noodleman

That Game From Outer Space:
The First Strange Thing That Happened to Oscar Noodleman

Video War

I'll Live

Be a Perfect Person in Just Three Days!

Socko!
Every Riddle Your Feet Will Ever Need

Pictures of Motion and Pictures That Move:
Eadweard Muybridge and the Photography of Motion

The Hooples' Haunted House

Slim Down Camp

The Boy Who Turned Into a TV Set

Hooples on the Highway

Mule in the Mail

WITH ESTHER MANES:
The Bananas Move to the Ceiling

The Second Strange Thing That Happened to Oscar Noodleman

The Oscar J. Noodleman Television Network

by Stephen Manes

illustrated by Roy Schlemme

E. P. DUTTON   NEW YORK

Edited by Weekly Reader Books. Published by
arrangement with E.P. Dutton, Inc.

Library of Congress Cataloging in Publication Data

Manes, Stephen, date
   The Oscar J. Noodleman television network.

   Summary: Soon after Oscar receives a home video
recorder and camera from his mother's eccentric inventor
cousin, Oscar's pictures begin to turn up mysteriously
on television sets all over town.
   [1. Video tape recorders and recording—Fiction.
2. Television broadcasting—Fiction.   3. Extraterrestrial
beings—Fiction]   I. Schlemme, Roy, ill.   II. Title.
PZ7.M3126405   1983   [Fic]   83-8970
ISBN 0-525-44075-5

Published in the United States by E. P. Dutton, Inc.,
2 Park Avenue, New York, N.Y. 10016

Published simultaneously in Canada by
Fitzhenry & Whiteside Limited, Toronto

Editor: Ann Durell   Designer: Isabel Warren-Lynch

Printed in the U.S.A.   COBE   First Edition
10 9 8 7 6 5 4 3 2 1

for Ann

1

Oscar Noodleman stormed out of the elevator with a very angry look on his face. "See you, stupid!" snorted Norval Molarsky.

"Not if I see you first!" Oscar shouted as the elevator doors closed. And he wasn't kidding.

Norval Molarsky was a worm, a slimeball, a genuine creep. Norval Molarsky was two hundred pounds of pure redheaded rottenness.

Norval Molarsky was the kind of person whose idea of fun was to steal rubber cement from the school storeroom and pour it all over the boys' room floor when you were in there minding your own business. If your shoes got stuck and a teacher

1

caught you and blamed you for the mess and sent you to the principal, Norval would think it was a riot. He'd laugh at you about it all the way home. In fact, Norval had just done all that to Oscar.

As he trudged down the hall to his apartment, Oscar kept muttering to himself. He'd get back at Norval somehow. He'd just have to. That was all there was to it. Somehow, Oscar told himself, someday . . .

Oh, what was the use? Norval was such an expert at practical jokes, dirty tricks, and evil deeds that nobody could think up one good enough to fool him. Nobody *ever* got back at Norval. Norval was just plain un-get-back-at-able.

As Oscar wiped his feet on the doormat, he noticed his sneakers were still kind of sticky. He was about to take them off when he spotted a messily scribbled note under the front door—a mysterious note that seemed to say *peck itchy left hand—furry Mess Cruller.*

2

Oscar squinted hard at the note. If his guess was right, *peck itchy left hand* had to mean "package left here." And *furry Mess Cruller* was almost certainly "for you—Mrs. Seltzer."

Oscar went next door and pressed Mrs. Seltzer's buzzer. "Who is it?" shrieked a voice as sweet as a chicken's.

"Oscar!" he hollered at the top of his lungs.

"Who is it?" the voice squawked back.

"Oscar!" Oscar shouted. "Oscar Noodleman!"

"Slip it under the door!" Mrs. Seltzer shouted.

Oscar sighed. He had been through this before. Mrs. Seltzer was slightly hard of hearing. You just had to be patient. "Mrs. Seltzer, it's me! Oscar!"

Oscar heard some shuffling behind the door. Then a suspicious eye peered out from the little peephole just above his head. "Is that you, Oscar Noodleman?"

"Yes," Oscar said.

"Well, why didn't you say so? You can't expect people to guess who you are!"

Oscar waited for Mrs. Seltzer to open all seven of her locks. Without undoing the last four chains, she opened the door an inch or two and squinted at him. "I guess you're Oscar, all right," she finally decided. "What do you want?"

"Did somebody bring us a package?"

Mrs. Seltzer looked puzzled. "Does my back itch? Sure does!"

Oscar sighed and asked his question again.

Mrs. Seltzer scratched her head. "Oh! *That!*" She unlatched the chains and flung open the door. There in her hallway was a box the size of a refrigerator, only taller—almost as tall as Mrs. Seltzer and Oscar put together.

A big **UP** was printed upside down on the box. So was a huge arrow that pointed straight to the floor. And the word **FRAGILE** was also printed upside down. In fact, the only rightside-up lettering on the enormous box was written by hand in bright blue capital letters. It said **TO: O. NOODLEMAN**.

Something had to be wrong. The packages that came to Oscar's apartment were always addressed to his parents. No one ever sent Oscar anything, except for his Aunt Mildred, who knitted him a lot of ugly sweaters like the one with bulldogs all over it that he was wearing right now. But this was definitely too big a package for an ugly sweater. In fact, it was too big a package for a lifetime supply of ugly sweaters.

"I bet it's a stuffed gorilla," Mrs. Seltzer declared.

"*I* bet it's a mistake," Oscar said. "It must be for some other O. Noodleman someplace else."

"Well, it's certainly not mine, and I don't want any stuffed gorillas monkeying up my place. You take it home and send it back if it's not for you."

Take it home? Oscar wasn't sure he could even

move it! A box that size had to weigh at least as much as a large ape.

"Well, go on," Mrs. Seltzer insisted. "I haven't got all week."

Oscar stood behind the box, leaned his shoulder against it, and pushed with all his might. Much to his surprise, the box almost sailed away. It wasn't exactly as light as a feather—but it wasn't much heavier than a huge box of them.

Mrs. Seltzer held the door open for him as he pushed the box into the hallway. "Take good care of your new gorilla," she told him. "And be careful you don't snag that beautiful sweater."

3

The first thing Oscar did when he got the box home was take off his sticky shoes. Then he got up on a chair to look at the top of the box. Just as he suspected: It had huge lettering that said **BOTTOM**.

He jumped down from the chair and tilted the box. Then he lowered it toward the floor as slowly and gently as he knew how.

Suddenly the cardboard slipped from his hands. The box crashed to the floor about as gracefully as a stuffed gorilla.

There was a loud thud, but he didn't hear anything break. And now he could see the bottom. He'd guessed right again: It was marked **TOP**.

Oscar went into the kitchen, brought back his mother's special package-opening scissors and got set to open the box. Then the phone rang.

Oscar answered it. A muffled voice on the other end of the line chortled obnoxiously and said, "Just wanted to talk to the most stuck-up kid in the neighborhood."

"Then talk to yourself," Oscar said, and hung up. Norval again. Something definitely had to be done about that guy.

But first something had to be done about the box. The heavy tape that sealed it was already broken in a dozen places. Oscar cut through what was left and gave one of the top flaps a mighty yank.

The box suddenly exploded with a silent puff of white plastic stuff that looked like popcorn. It kept spilling into the room as though it might never stop.

Oscar knew how much his mother hated plastic popcorn, but he decided he'd clean it up later. First he had to find out what was inside the box. Crawling in cautiously—he didn't want to find a *live* gorilla staring back at him—he pawed through the popcorn avalanche until he found something else.

It was an imitation leather case about the size of a briefcase—only a lot heavier. It felt as though there must be some kind of machine inside.

Oscar dragged the case out of the box. Attached to the front was a big blue notebook. In huge red handwritten letters, the cover shouted:

WARNING

DO NOT USE
BEFORE **COMPLETELY** READING THESE
INSTRUCTIONS.*

At the very bottom, Oscar saw this notice:

*No kidding!

Oscar lifted up the cover and read the first page of the notebook.

Welcome to the wonderful world of
THE PRECHTWINKLE VIDEO RECORDER
Your passport to viewing pleasure!

Totally astounded, Oscar opened the imitation leather case. There in front of him was a round

metallic green machine with tiny red buttons on it.
It looked like Christmas. It looked like fun.

And there was no doubt about it now. The package couldn't possibly be for him. Nobody would ever send a kid like Oscar a snazzy new video recorder out of the blue like this. Nobody would even think about it.

On the other hand, there couldn't be any harm in trying it out.

4

THE PRECHTWINKLE VIDEO RECORDER

(said the instruction notebook)

is
the most amazing machine
the world has ever seen!
Really!

THE PRECHTWINKLE VIDEO RECORDER
turns your TV set
into
A HOME ENTERTAINMENT PALACE!

Now you can watch your favorite shows whenever you want to—and you can watch them again and again. But that's not all. You can watch them:

- in slow motion
- in fast motion
- in super-slow motion
- in super-fast motion
- forward
- backward
- inside out
- upside down
- sideways

or any combination at once! Imagine watching your favorite programs upside down and backward in super-fast motion. Not only would you know right away how the program came out, but you could also do headstands and other healthful exercises without missing a thing. To top it off, you'd also save valuable time that you could use for important things—like trimming your toenails.

But we haven't begun to tell you all the things THE PRECHTWINKLE VIDEO RECORDER can do for you. We'd rather show you. So turn the pages and get ready for enjoyment.

Oscar read the step-by-step instructions. They couldn't have been simpler. To turn the machine on or off, you pressed the ON / OFF button. To record a program, you pressed the RECORD button. To play a program back, you rewound the tape with the REWIND button and then played it with the PLAY button. You could do any of those things from across

13

the room with a little remote control gizmo. And you didn't even have to hook up the recorder to your television set. All you had to do was plug it in, and it would do the rest.

"No! No!" shrieked a voice from the hallway. Ten seconds later Oscar's mother appeared at his bedroom door with a pile of white plastic popcorn cupped in one hand and a very grim look on her face.

"Oscar, what is the meaning of this?"

"Huh?"

"There is white plastic popcorn all over the hallway. It is attacking the living room. It is my least favorite substance in the entire world, with the possible exception of bathtub rings. What do you intend to do about it?"

"I'll clean it up, Mom. In a minute."

"You certainly will. You will also take that enormous box down to the basement so we have room to walk in here. And what in the world are we going to do with a stuffed gorilla?"

"What stuffed gorilla?"

"I ran into Mrs. Seltzer on the elevator. She said somebody sent you a stuffed gorilla."

"Mrs. Seltzer got a little confused."

"Then what was in the box?"

"You are never going to believe it," Oscar said.

"A stuffed rhinoceros?" his mother asked suspiciously.

"Not even close."

"A stuffed turkey?" she asked hopefully.

"Not quite."

His mother looked around the room. "Oh, no!" she shrieked. "Not a home video recorder!"

Oscar's jaw dropped open. "How'd you ever guess?"

His mother shook her head back and forth angrily. "I told that cousin of mine not to send you that machine. But did he listen? Ha!"

"Your cousin sent me this?"

Mrs. Noodleman sighed. "I'm afraid so. His name is Dr. Peter Prechtwinkle. I haven't seen him in years. He invents things."

"What kinds of things?"

"Things like this video recorder, I guess."

"Why did he send it to *me*?"

"Your guess is as good as mine. He phoned a few

days ago. He said he was going on vacation and he wanted somebody to try it out for a couple of weeks. I told him absolutely not—and look what happened! All I have to say is *Grrrrr!* Back it goes!"

"Come on, Mom. It looks neat."

His mother frowned.

"I won't watch too much TV with it," Oscar said. "Honest."

Oscar's mother scowled. His parents hated television. They never watched it themselves, and they insisted it would rot your mind. The only TV in the house was the one in Oscar's room, and he had to promise not to watch it more than one hour a day except on special occasions. He hardly ever cheated, since there wasn't all that much he wanted to watch anyhow except during baseball season.

"Please?" Oscar begged. "I promise."

Oscar's mother's look turned more suspicious than ever. "Well, I suppose," she said. "If your father agrees. But you'd better be careful with that machine. It's only on loan. You have to send it back when my cousin gets home from his vacation."

"Oh," Oscar sighed. It didn't seem fair somehow. It was kind of like winning a prize that would turn into a squash at midnight.

"And I hope he explained to you that it's a special machine," said his mother. "It's experimental. There's not another one like it in the entire world."

Oscar suddenly felt a goose-bumpy shiver run down his spine. The only other thing he owned that

16

was the only one like it in the entire world was a baseball signed by two of the Wartburg Whitecaps, and if something went wrong with that, nobody would know it but him, since he didn't have to give it back. "What if the recorder breaks?" he asked.

"Then, my dear boy, you are in big trouble. Still want to keep it?"

"I guess so," Oscar squeaked.

5

Carefully following the instructions, Oscar took a tape cassette from the case and put it in a slot. The recorder swallowed the cassette. Then it said, "Thank you. I'm ready now."

Maybe he was imagining it. The instructions hadn't mentioned a word about the machine being able to talk. Oscar pressed the EJECT button, took out the cassette, and put the cassette back in the slot. The machine swallowed it up again and said, "Thank you. I'm ready now."

"Me, too, especially for dinner," announced Oscar's father as he came through the bedroom door. "Oscar, what happened out in the hallway? A late spring snowstorm?"

Mrs. Noodleman came in to greet him. "My delightful Cousin Peter sent Oscar a video recorder," she said in a way that sounded as though she didn't think her Cousin Peter was the least bit delightful.

"In a box that size?" Mr. Noodleman asked. "For a minute there, I thought somebody'd sent us a stuffed gorilla."

"This is going to be a lot better than a stuffed gorilla," said Oscar.

"If it has anything to do with television, I would tend to doubt it," said Mr. Noodleman, examining the new machine as though it might bite him. "Is Peter that cousin of yours who invents things?" he asked his wife.

"I'm afraid so," said she.

"What else did he invent besides this video recorder?" Oscar wanted to know.

Mrs. Noodleman looked thoughtful. "I'm not quite sure. I believe he developed some of those little magnetic clips that you stick notes up on refrigerators with. I think he invented one that looked like a mango. Or maybe it was a banjo."

"An invention that changed the world!" snorted Mr. Noodleman.

"This one does seem a little more interesting," Oscar agreed.

"Not to me," said Mr. Noodleman. "Anything connected with television can cause mind rot in thirty seconds." And he walked out the door with Oscar's mother right behind him.

Oscar followed the directions in the notebook.

19

First he pressed the big red RECORD button on the front of the Prechtwinkle Video Recorder. Then he turned on the TV set. A talk show appeared on the screen.

"Well, Gerb," said a tall blonde woman with eyelashes almost as long as her nose, "after my big success in *That Sure Is Stupid!*, you could hardly expect me to do something less dignified. But it took me a long time to find a truly worthwhile role."

"And now, Griselda Wockenfuss, you're starring in your very own movie," gushed Gerb, the host. "*Apes Go Wild*, right?"

"Yes, Gerb, isn't it thrilling? To me and the rest of our great cast, it is a true challenge to play the role of a gorilla. To make people really feel for these wonderful creatures was my most difficult acting assignment ever."

She had brought along a clip from the film. The host told the studio audience to watch the monitors.

Ten gorillas suddenly went crazy on the screen. They chased a hunter through the jungle. Then they shook their fists at the camera and chanted "Ugga! Bugga! Ugga! Bugga!" It was not exactly the best job of acting Oscar had ever seen. In fact, it might well have been the worst. The movie was so bad you could see the zippers in the gorilla suits.

"Griselda," said Gerb, flashing all ninety-seven of his teeth, "if you ask my opinion, this could very well be your finest, most important role. The acting you did in that scene is simply amazing." The audience applauded in agreement.

"Thank you, Gerb, thank you," said Griselda modestly.

Enough was enough. Oscar could almost feel his mind rotting. Following the instructions in the notebook ever so carefully, he pressed the REWIND button. The machine made a faint whirring noise, and he could see tape moving in a little window.

Then he pressed the button marked PLAY. The screen went blank for a long, long second.

Suddenly Gerb and Griselda told the studio audience to watch the monitors. The gorillas went crazy again. They shouted "Ugga! Bugga!" again. It was exactly like the first time, right down to the zippers. The Prechtwinkle Video Recorder actually worked!

Oscar pressed the button marked REVERSE. The gorillas began running backward and went "!agguB !aggU !agguB !aggU"

Oscar pressed the SLOW button. The gorillas floated backward like hairy ballet dancers. Oscar pressed the STOP button, and they stopped in mid-air.

He tried the button marked SUPERSPEED. The fake gorillas made noises like chipmunks and ran forward so fast Oscar thought their suits might fall off. Then he pressed REVERSE. The gorillas ran backward even faster and sounded like munkchips. Oscar pressed UPSIDE DOWN, and the gorillas dangled from the top of the screen as they ran.

"Oscar!" his mother called from the living room. "Clean up all that plastic popcorn and take that big box downstairs to the garbage room this instant! I will not eat dinner in the same apartment with a blizzard of plastic popcorn!"

Oscar could think of about eight million things he would rather do than take the box downstairs, but he knew his mother's serious tone when he heard it. He put on a glueless pair of shoes, went out into the living room, and stuffed the popcorn back into the box. Then he dragged the box out the door and down the hallway. He pressed the elevator button and waited.

The door opened. Oscar shoved the box into the elevator and rode down to the basement. As usual, the garbage room was locked. This was to keep people from accidentally falling into the trash compactor and being crunched to death and complaining to the landlord about it afterwards. Oscar left the box outside the door.

Oscar sighed as he got back into the elevator and rode upstairs. He felt slightly disappointed, kind of like the time a friend of his had swapped him a set of false teeth that wound up and clacked across the kitchen table. At first it had seemed pretty neat, but he'd ended up trading it for two second-rate comic books.

It was almost the same with the video recorder. Somehow he wasn't really as thrilled about it as he thought he'd be. Seeing gorillas and even people run around backward and in slow motion was fun for a while, but he had the feeling he'd get tired of it pretty fast. Yet he couldn't trade the video recorder, since he had to give it back. There had to be something else it could do. Something interesting. Something fun.

Back in the apartment, Oscar picked up the instruction notebook and paged through it again. He had read it from cover to cover, and he was sure he hadn't missed anything, but he decided to read it through one more time. Then he noticed some tiny print at the very bottom of the last page. It said:

If you have THE PRECHTWINKLE VIDEO CAMERA, be sure to read Manual 001-C.

Oscar sat up with a start and ran out of the room. A camera! Of course! That's what was missing!

As he zoomed down the hallway and pressed the elevator button, Oscar hoped he wasn't too late. He could just see it now: his brand-new Prechtwinkle Video Camera, the only one in the entire world, squashed flat into a tiny little garbage pancake! What would his mother's cousin have to say about that?

6

The camera could get mashed in the trash any second. But the elevator seemed to be taking forever to show up. Oscar pressed the button again. But he knew it wouldn't help.

Suddenly the doors opened. Norval Molarsky was standing there with his pet mongrel Fluffles, the world's ugliest dog. Norval took one look at Oscar, pretended his shoes were stuck to the floor, and howled with laughter. That was Norval for you. He never let up. Not ever.

Oscar was tempted to wait for the next elevator, but he had to get that camera back. The second he stepped inside, Fluffles began gnawing the left leg

of his jeans. Fluffles had taken a course in obnox-
iousness from an expert. The harder Oscar tried to
kick him away, the harder Fluffles held on, growling
and drooling.

"Will you get your dog off of me?" Oscar
screamed.

Norval said not a word.

"Norval, you jerk!" Oscar hollered as Fluffles began working on his sock. "Get this mutt to stop!"

Norval just grinned. Fluffles growled and
drooled some more. Oscar wished he owned a *live*
gorilla—a man-eating one that occasionally nibbled
on dogs.

The elevator stopped at the lobby. Norval
snapped his fingers, and Fluffles stomped out behind him. The doors closed, and Oscar began thinking about the squashed camera again. Just the
thought was even worse than running into Norval
and Fluffles. It was bad enough being damp at the
ankles from Fluffles' drool, but now Oscar also felt
sick to his stomach.

The elevator stopped at the basement. Oscar
rushed out and dashed around the corner. The
huge box was nowhere to be seen.

Then Oscar noticed the garbage room door was
open a crack. "Hey! Wait!" he yelled.

"Hey? Wait?" a voice with a heavy foreign accent
called back from behind the door.

Oscar knew that voice. It was Emil, the porter—the person who took the garbage and mashed it in the compactor.

"Yes!" Oscar shouted frantically. "Wait!" He flung the door open and ran into the garbage room.

The huge box was on the floor right in front of the trash compactor. Emil was standing beside it. "Yes?" he said.

"That box!" Oscar gasped. "There's something in it!"

"You telling me? I see plastic popcorn all the time in stuff people throw away, but that box gots more in one place than I ever see before."

Oscar felt his knees quaking. "What did you do with it?" he squeaked.

"I dump in the compactor," Emil said proudly. "No more popcorn."

"Oh," said Oscar, feeling sicker by the second.

"Soon I break box into little pieces so it fits too. You want to help, maybe?"

"N-no," Oscar stammered. "I mean, that box belongs to me. I didn't mean to leave it down here."

"Here! Take back!" said Emil, shoving the box in Oscar's direction. "Will save me trouble of tearing into little pieces."

"Yes, but . . ."

"Now watch. Very interesting. Compactor turns popcorn into nice little lump."

"Wait!" Oscar tried to shout, but all that came out was a tiny little croak. Before Oscar could make another sound, Emil gave a loving tug on a big red lever. With a loud grunt, the door to the machine swung closed. Then an even louder *WHOMP!* announced that the compactor was working.

"Some machine, huh?" Emil said with great pride.

The compactor made a loud crunching noise. Oscar could hear glass breaking and metal grinding —exactly the sounds a camera would make if it were being crushed by thousands of pounds of pressure. He was sure he was going to throw up.

Emil turned off the machine. "I have to close up now," he said. "You want to take your box, please?"

Oscar let out a deep sigh. What was the use? The camera was gone, gone forever. He certainly didn't want the box around to remind him. "You may as well start ripping it up," he said. "It's no good to me now."

"You sure?" Emil asked.

"Yes," Oscar sighed.

"Okay," Emil said. "You sure you don't want to help?"

"Positive," Oscar said.

"Then maybe you want to watch."

"Not really," Oscar said.

Emil just shrugged. With a mighty yank, he ripped

one side of the box all the way down one side. Then he yanked again, and the box came apart.

Suddenly Oscar noticed something at the very bottom. Resting on half a dozen stray pieces of plastic popcorn was a black imitation leather case about half the size of the one the recorder had come in!

Oscar couldn't believe his eyes. "You said you dumped everything into the compactor."

Emil's eyes twinkled a little. "I say I dump plastic stuff into compactor. I don't say nothing about something somebody might have left in box by accident."

Oscar carefully set the camera on a table. Just to make absolutely sure nothing was left inside the box, he crawled in and had a careful look around. Finally he crawled out again. "Okay," he told Emil happily. "Rip away!"

7

Oscar set the camera case on his bed and opened it. Inside the case was another notebook. The cover said **USER'S MANUAL—THE PRECHTWINKLE VIDEO CAMERA, MODEL X-ONE.** It also said **DON'T BE STUPID! READ ALL INSTRUCTIONS FIRST!**

He took out the camera. It was a greenish color that matched the recorder. It had a big lens on the front and a microphone on top. The handle on the bottom fit perfectly into Oscar's hand. The camera even smelled good.

And it was as easy to use as the recorder. Maybe even easier. All you really had to do was turn it on and look through the viewfinder, which was like a tiny TV set. When it showed what you wanted to

31

shoot, you just pressed a button. The signal would go straight through the air to the recorder. If you wanted to, you could even send the signal the other way and play your tapes back through the camera's TV viewfinder.

Oscar couldn't wait to try it out. Peering at the viewfinder, he snuck into the living room. His mother was reading the evening paper and picking her nose.

She stopped picking her nose and scowled at Oscar. "Oscar, are you taking pictures of me?"

Oscar giggled. "Sort of."

"Then sort of cut it out."

"Just pretend I'm not here."

"Out," said Oscar's mother. "Begone. Scat. Depart."

Oscar took the hint. He pointed the camera at his father, who was snoozing on the couch.

Mr. Noodleman woke up with a start. "Well, that's just dandy," he snapped. "The camera makes it perfect. A complete Mind Rot Kit. Can't even snore in peace. Let me see that thing."

Oscar handed it to him. "Be careful."

Mr. Noodleman frowned. "How do I turn it on?"

Oscar showed him.

"Oho!" cried Mr. Noodleman. "There's a little TV set in there."

"That's the viewfinder," Oscar said professionally.

"So it is. You know what that means, don't you?"

Oscar looked puzzled.

"It means that if you're using the camera, you're watching television. So remember: One hour with the camera is the same as one hour with the TV set. We don't need any rotten minds around here."

"Mom?" Oscar pleaded.

"We'll see," said his mother. It did not sound promising.

Oscar went back to his bedroom. He walked around and pointed the camera at various things, but he couldn't find anything worth shooting. He aimed at the goldfish, but the goldfish were asleep. He aimed at his schoolbooks, but he had to admit they weren't terribly exciting. He aimed at a neat poster of a space station on his wall, but even through the camera it still looked more like a poster than a space station. The best idea he could come up with was to aim at his TV set. That way he got a picture of himself taking a picture of himself taking a picture of himself . . . which was actually pretty interesting. But not for long.

He pointed the camera out his window. The street below was full of people coming home from work. At the newsstand, a bearded businessman in a three-piece suit was fumbling in his pocket for change. In front of the delicatessen, a short, sweaty delivery-man with muscles like small mountains was lifting a case of pickles onto each shoulder. Further up the street, a redheaded woman was walking her fluffy white cats. It was more interesting than Oscar's space station poster, but not by much.

Oscar zoomed the lens in for a closer look. An

extremely fat lady came out of the bakery chomping on a huge cookie. Then Oscar spotted a kid he thought he recognized. He zoomed closer. It was the jerk Norval, coming out of the ice-cream store with a triple-decker cone in his hand. Fluffles was waiting for him beside the fireplug.

Just one look reminded Oscar how much he hated Norval. And it gave him an idea. Sooner or later, Norval would probably do something mean and rotten, the way he usually did. If Oscar kept the camera on Norval, he would have it on tape. And he might be able to use the tape to get back at Norval somehow. Oscar pressed the RECORD button on the camera and hoped something truly nasty would happen. All that happened was that Norval leaned against the fireplug.

The pickle man wobbled under his load as he carried it from the truck toward the delicatessen. Suddenly Norval grabbed Fluffles' leash and slapped the dog on the rear end. Fluffles ran straight across the sidewalk, stretching the leash out tight right in front of the deliveryman—who went flying across the pavement.

Pickle jars sailed every which way and crashed to the sidewalk, shattering and exploding. The fat lady with the cookie tiptoed around some broken glass and slipped on a kosher dill. The businessman's beard dripped pickle juice. The two white cats turned greenish. And Norval and Fluffles laughed and laughed until the deliveryman shook his fist at them.

Oscar's camera captured it all. He decided to quit shooting and see if everything got recorded on the tape. He turned off the camera and pressed the RE-WIND button on the video recorder. Then he pressed PLAY.

Sure enough, there on the TV screen was his mother picking her nose. There was his father snoring on the couch. There were the ice-cream store and Norval and Fluffles and the deliveryman and the pickles. Oscar played it all backwards, which made it even funnier in a cruel sort of way.

He stuck his camera out the window again. Maybe something even better would happen. Maybe there'd be a robbery or something over at the bank, and his camera could save the day. Or maybe a meteorite would land smack in the middle of the street, preferably on Norval's head. But nothing much was going on. Aside from the pickle-juice lake and gherkin islands in the middle of the sidewalk, everything had gone back to normal.

Oscar went back inside, rewound the tape again, and tried playing it back through the camera's little

TV viewfinder. All he had to do was press the PLAY button on the camera. It worked just fine. It even worked in slow motion. The equipment was really kind of neat. Now if only he could use it to get back at the rottenest kid in the neighborhood, everything would be perfect.

"What's shakin'?" Norval snarled at Oscar as he got on the elevator the next morning.

Oscar just shrugged. He decided not to mention a word about his new video equipment. Norval would be sure to think of something terrible to do with it—something a lot worse than crushing it to death in the compactor.

"My parents are ticked off again," Norval grumped.

"What'd you do this time?" Oscar asked.

"I didn't do anything. I was out walking Fluffles, and I went for an ice cream."

"That doesn't sound so terrible," Oscar agreed.

"Yeah, well, I wasn't supposed to go for an ice cream. They were like punishing me because I accidentally on purpose put hot sauce in their oatmeal yesterday morning."

"It figures," said Oscar.

"Yeah, but I made sure to go to that place on your side of the building. We don't have any windows on that side, so they couldn't look out and check up on me."

"Then how'd they find out?" Oscar asked.

"That's the weird part. They said they saw me on TV. They said they were watching the news, and then right in the middle, all these weird programs came on. First this lady was picking her nose."

"Huh?"

"I didn't see it. I'm just telling you what they told me. Then there was this guy snoring."

The program was beginning to sound very familiar. "Weird," Oscar muttered.

"I'll say. Then there was this program where you saw the street and people were just walking along. Really boring. But just when they were about to change the channel, they saw me coming out of the ice-cream store. *Real* weird, huh?"

Oscar kept his mouth shut. He just nodded.

"They also saw how Fluffles and I made this guy drop two whole cases of pickles! They went all over the place. I mean, pickles everywhere! It was a riot! Funniest thing you ever saw."

"I bet," said Oscar.

39

"But my parents didn't think it was so funny. They got real mad. I had to go to bed without supper. Big deal. I just ate a couple pounds of stuff from my secret candy hideout."

Oscar couldn't figure it out. His camera couldn't really be sending out pictures to other people's TV sets. It had to be some sort of crazy coincidence.

"What I wonder," Norval grunted, "is who the sneak was who took pictures of me when I wasn't looking. I'd like to meet up with him in a back alley sometime." He punched his left fist into his right hand for emphasis. Oscar felt slightly uncomfortable.

Mandy caught up with them as she came out of her building. "Hey, Norval!" she shouted. "I saw you on TV last night!"

"No kidding?" said Norval.

"Yeah," said Mandy. "You and Fluffles tripped this guy who was delivering a load of pickles."

"What channel was it on?" Oscar asked.

"I think it was on 7," Mandy said. "I was watching this mystery show, and right when they were going to tell you who did it, this weird program came on. It started with this woman picking her nose. I thought it was a commercial at first, but it went on too long. Later on they showed the street, and then they showed Norval making this delivery guy drop a whole load of pickles. They even showed it in slow motion."

"I wonder who else saw it," said Norval. "It sure is weird to turn up on television like that when all you're doing is minding your own business."

"Sure is," said Mandy. "I wonder if there'll be any more shows like that."

Oscar shuddered slightly. "You never can tell."

All the way to school, Norval was the focus of attention. Almost everyone had seen him on TV the night before. Some kids saw him in the middle of comedy programs. Some saw him in the middle of commercials. Some saw him in the middle of the news. One kid even saw him in the middle of a program about electric eels. Norval seemed to have been on all the channels at the same time, around six-thirty, precisely when Oscar was fooling around with the camera.

"Class," said Oscar's homeroom teacher, " we

seem to have a television star among us today. Norval, can you explain what you were doing on the six o'clock news?"

Norval grinned. "I won an award for good behavior," he said.

Everyone howled with laughter. Everyone but Oscar and the teacher. The teacher was busy disposing of a small dead rat that Norval had stuck in her roll book. And Oscar was busy wondering about his new video equipment.

If it really could send out pictures to the entire neighborhood, he could start his own television station. And then there'd be no telling what he could do. Someday soon the entire world might be tuning in to the Oscar J. Noodleman Television Network!

Oscar paid absolutely no attention in class all day. He couldn't wait to get home and figure out what was going on. He knew he would have to tell somebody. And if there was one person who could help him with video stuff, it was definitely his friend Donald.

Donald had his own TV set, his own video game machine, his own computer, his own video disc player, and his own video recorder. In fact, Donald had dozens of things Oscar wished he had. But basically Donald was all right. The only trouble with Donald was that he was rich.

Donald didn't go to public school like Oscar did. He took a limousine to some private school for rich

43

kids way uptown. Donald lived across the street from Oscar in the tall new building at the corner, the one with a canopy over the doorway and a doorman at the entrance and gold chandeliers in the lobby. It was quite a bit fancier than Oscar's lobby, which only had an old broken chair Emil liked to sit in when he wasn't busy.

"Why don't you come over here?" Donald said when Oscar phoned. "I just got this great new video game cartridge. In this one, you're the monster, and you get to stomp human beings."

"I've got something even better," Oscar told him.

"I also got this great new record," Donald went on. "It sounds like a whole flock of chickens singing famous country songs."

"Come on, Donald, I was over at your place last time. And the time before that. And the time before that."

"That's because I keep getting all this neat stuff."

"Well, this time I've got something pretty amazing."

"What?"

"It's a surprise."

"How big a surprise?"

"Come on, Donald. It's your turn to come here."

"How big a surprise?" he repeated. "I had a hard day at school. I'm not going to put on my shoes, and go out the door, and take the elevator downstairs and walk over to your place and take the elevator upstairs and do all that unless it's worth it."

"It's worth it," Oscar said.

44

"Prove it."

"What if I told you the world's scariest monster was climbing up the side of my building, and three of its tentacles were already sticking through my living room window?"

"I'll be right over," Donald said, and hung up. Donald was the world's greatest authority on monsters. He had seen almost every monster movie ever filmed, he built model monsters in his spare time, and if you were willing to talk about monsters with him, he would go anywhere. He and Oscar had made an agreement: Whenever it was super-urgent to get together, they would pretend there was a monster attack. Monster attacks were something Donald took very seriously.

Five minutes later there was a buzz from the intercom. Oscar pressed the TALK button and asked, "Who is it?"

"The Creature from the Black Lagoon," said the voice on the other end. Oscar pressed a different button and let the Creature into the building.

One minute later the door buzzer rang. Oscar got up on tiptoe, looked through the little peephole the way his parents said he was supposed to, and saw Donald sticking his tongue out at him. Oscar opened the door.

"Well, this better be good," Donald said. "This neat movie about jellyfish invading South Dakota is on TV in half an hour."

"You can watch it here."

"No offense, Osc, but I would rather watch it on

a ten-foot video screen than on that dinky TV your parents bought you. Monsters are a lot scarier when they're bigger. Now, where's this monster of yours?"

"Come on in the bedroom," Oscar said.

They went into the bedroom. "So where's the monster?" Donald demanded.

"Headed downtown. He's probably a couple of blocks away by now."

Donald snapped his fingers in dismay. "Darn! I always seem to just miss them!" He and Oscar both smiled. "Okay, Osc, what's the big surprise?"

Oscar went to his dresser and picked up the video camera. "This!" he said proudly.

Donald just shrugged. "What's the big deal? It's a video camera. My grandparents have one. Every once in a while they bring it out and take pictures of me and my sister at a birthday party or a bar mitzvah or something."

"I'll bet theirs isn't like this."

Donald came in for a closer look. "Nah, theirs has a Japanese name. I've never heard of a Prechtwinkle."

"That's because my mom's cousin invented it."

"Come on, Oscar. Stop with the mystery. Only twenty-five minutes till monster time."

Oscar looked at him through the camera. "What would you say if I told you that if I took your picture with this camera right now, people all through my building would be able to watch you?"

"I'd say you were as nutty as a pecan pie."

"What would you say if I told you I could take pictures with this camera and send them all across the neighborhood?"

"I'd say you were as nutty as two pecan pies."

"What would you say if I told you I could shoot you now with this camera, record it on tape, and then when you got home I could play it back on my new video recorder and you would see yourself on your TV set?"

"I'd say you were as nutty as a whole pecan pie factory!"

"Well, you'd better say it, then, because it's all true."

"Come on, Oscar. Don't kid me. That's about as true as the monster outside your window."

"I'm not kidding, Donald. This is for real." And Oscar told him all about his parents and Norval and how they had turned up on all the TV sets in the neighborhood.

"They didn't turn up on *my* TV set last night," Donald said.

Oscar looked thoughtful. "Maybe you didn't have it on."

"Come to think of it, I was uptown having dinner at a restaurant," said Donald. "Tanzanian roast ostrich in Australian kiwi fruit sauce over Chinese noodles, with Belgian endive and Canadian bacon. Guatemalan coffee and Baked Alaska for dessert."

Sometimes Donald and his money could be a real pain. "Just another boring meal, I guess," said Oscar.

"Very funny. I can't help it if my folks are rich. And I still don't believe this craziness about your video recorder."

"Well, you're wrong."

Donald looked at his expensive watch. "It's only ten minutes till show time. I want to get home and tape this movie on my video recorder. Enough jokes about your camera. Want to come over and watch?"

"What if I prove I can send pictures to your TV?"

"Ha!"

Oscar put the camera to his eye. "Pretend you're a monster jellyfish," he told Donald.

"Huh?" Donald said.

"Like the one you're going home to watch. Come

on! Pretend you're about to invade South Dakota!"

Oscar pressed the RECORD button on the camera and looked at the tiny picture of Donald in the viewfinder. He moved closer and closer as Donald twisted up his face and pulled in his neck and shoulders and generally made his whole body a blob. He didn't look much like a jellyfish, but he did look pretty disgusting. The horrible blob monster made strange little snorting noises and lunged at the camera, ready to attack.

"Help! Help!" Oscar cried as Donald's sickening monster face filled up every inch of the tiny screen, looking like it was about to swallow him. Then he turned off the camera.

Donald turned back into a human being again. "Well?" he demanded.

"Well what?" Oscar said calmly. "You'd better get home in a hurry. You don't want to miss your movie."

10

The minute Donald went through the door, Oscar picked up the remote control for the video recorder, rewound his latest tape, and played it back. Donald made a terrific monster, especially near the end, where it really did look as though he might swallow the lens again. Oscar pressed the REWIND button and wound the tape back to the beginning.

Meanwhile he tuned the TV to the channel where Donald's monster movie was supposed to be. First there was an ad for tomorrow's monster movie, *Man-Eating Cauliflower.* Then a commercial for vegetable sauce showed a grumpy woman eating turnips and a delighted man eating cauliflower.

Finally *The Afternoon Fright* came on. There was a

lot of spooky music, and a picture of a deserted beach, and finally the title: *The Jellyfish That Stung South Dakota*.

It was the moment Oscar had been waiting for. The instant the title left the screen, he pressed the PLAY button on the recorder's remote control. What appeared next was Donald the Jellyfish attacking South Dakota—or at least the camera. When the ferocious attack ended, Oscar pressed the STOP button, and the movie came back on.

Oscar rocked back and forth impatiently in his chair. He was sure the minute Donald saw himself on TV, he would pick up the phone and call. But five minutes went by, and there was still no word from Donald.

Oscar figured Donald might be waiting until the commercials came on so that he wouldn't miss any of the movie. But six commercials came and went, and the giant jellyfish (which looked suspiciously like spaghetti and meatballs) began slithering across the prairie. Oscar's phone remained remarkably silent.

Oscar couldn't wait any longer. He went out to the living room, picked up the phone, and dialed Donald's number. The telephone rang exactly nine times. Oscar was ready to hang up when Donald finally answered.

"Well, did you see it?" Oscar demanded.

"Oscar, I told you, I do not believe that story of yours even a little bit. And I am trying to watch this movie. So if you want to talk, call me later, okay?"

"You mean, you didn't see yourself?"

"Come on, Oscar, give me a break. This is a rare movie. They only run it once every five or six years, and I don't want to miss it."

"But you're getting it on tape," Oscar said. "You can watch it anytime."

"I've told you a million times, it's not the same. Talk to you later." Donald hung up.

Oscar couldn't figure it out. Maybe Donald's building couldn't get the signal for some peculiar reason. But maybe something else was going wrong now, and *nobody* was getting a signal from Oscar's machine.

Well, there was one easy way to find out. There was no doubt that Norval would be watching the jellyfish movie, too. Norval liked monster movies a lot. He sympathized with the monsters. He rooted for them. Oscar picked up the phone and dialed his number.

"Yeah?" Norval answered through what sounded like a mouthful of potato chips.

"It's me—Oscar! Are you watching that jellyfish movie?"

"None of your beeswax."

"I just want to know if you're watching it."

"What else would I be doing? My homework?" Norval brayed a nasty laugh that made Oscar very glad that half-chewed potato chips could not come through the phone.

Oscar put one hand over his free ear. He could hear the jellyfish making slimy noises in the background at Norval's. "Listen," Oscar asked, "did you see anything unusual at the beginning of the film?"

"Well, it isn't every day you see a twenty-foot-wide jellyfish."

"That's not what I meant. Did you see anything that looked like it wasn't supposed to be there? Like the way everybody saw you on TV last night?"

"Yeah. I saw a fruit fly land on the screen."

"Come on, Norval. Get serious."

"Nah, all I saw was jellyfish."

"Okay. Just checking."

"Why? Did you see something weird on your tube?" Norval demanded.

"Well, it isn't every day you see a twenty-foot-wide jellyfish."

"Okay for you, creep. I'll see you tomorrow. I want to find out what happens to South Dakota." And he hung up.

Oscar was more confused than ever. As thousands of South Dakotans screamed "It's a giant jellyfish!" on the TV screen, he lay down on his bed to think.

He leafed through the two manuals for the recorder and the camera. He thought about how he'd taped things the night before and how he'd shot them with the camera.

Then it hit him.

He rewound the tape to the beginning of Donald's monstrous performance. Then he picked up the camera and pressed its PLAY button. In the camera's little TV viewfinder, he saw Donald lurching toward him with his strange jellyfish-like gait. And then Donald attacked.

Ten seconds later the telephone rang. It was Donald. "I'll be right over," he said.

11

Donald was at Oscar's door faster than you can say *The Jellyfish That Stung South Dakota* a dozen times.

"Now do you believe me?" Oscar said as he looked through the peephole.

"Of course I believe you," Donald said. "Let me in."

Oscar did.

"Is anybody else home now?" Donald asked in a very secret tone.

"No," said Oscar as they went to his bedroom.

"Did you tell anybody else about this?" Donald asked.

"Well, I didn't really *tell* anyone," Oscar replied.

Donald looked hurt. "What do you mean?"

"I mean, a lot of people saw Norval on TV last night."

"Oh, yeah," said Donald. "I forgot. But nobody knows where those pictures came from, right?"

"Nope," Oscar said. "Just you and me."

"Then it should be easy."

"What should be easy?"

"To fool everybody in the neighborhood."

"Huh?"

"Didn't you ever hear about *War of the Worlds*?" Oscar shook his head.

"It was just about the biggest scare anybody ever had, that's all. It was back before there was television, and this guy named Orson Welles did it on the radio. It was around Halloween night. First there was this program of music. Then all of a sudden there were these news reports that huge creatures from another planet had just landed in a farm in New Jersey. Well, then they went back to the music, but a couple of seconds later the reports came on again. There was a news bulletin direct from the farm, and the reporter said these aliens were heading for New York City."

"Come on," Oscar said. "Who would believe anything like that?"

"Everybody!" Donald replied with a wicked glint in his eye. "In fact, right in the middle of the show, they even said that it was just a play, that it wasn't real. But a lot of people didn't listen. All across the country, they left their houses and tried to get away before the Martians or whatever they were got there. People ran around in the streets and got all panicked. Some people even thought it was the end of the world. Was it ever neat! I've got a record of the program. You can listen to it sometime if you want."

"Sounds okay," Oscar admitted.

"It was a lot better than okay," said Donald. "It was fabulous. And I bet we can do something even better."

Oscar began to see what Donald had in mind.

"The way you describe it," Donald went on, "we can send out programs to the whole neighborhood, right? Anybody who's watching TV will see whatever we put out on the air?"

"Yeah, but . . ."

"So we can do some programs that'll fool people."

"People don't get fooled that easily."

"That's where you're wrong. Fooling people is the easiest thing in the world. And I know just how to do it."

"I don't know," Oscar said. "Maybe we'll get in trouble."

"Trouble? Of course we won't get in trouble. If anything, we'll be famous. Look what happened to Orson Welles."

"What happened?" Oscar asked.

"Come on. He's that fat guy with the deep voice

who does all those commercials. Like that one for wine."

Oscar wasn't sure that he really wanted to end up being fat and doing wine commercials. But at least it was nice to know that Orson Welles wasn't in jail for fooling people.

"People love to be fooled. Look at magicians. People pay to see them, even though they know they're being fooled."

"Yeah, but you're not just talking about fooling people. You're talking about *scaring* them."

"People even pay to be scared," said Donald. "They go on roller coasters. They go to scary movies."

Suddenly a fiendish thought ran through Oscar's brain. He wasn't all that interested in frightening the entire neighborhood. But there was one person that he wouldn't mind scaring clean out of his skull.

"Do you think we could do something that would really scare Norval?" Oscar asked.

"That dope? Easiest thing in the world," Donald said confidently.

"How?" Oscar asked.

Donald's face broke into a diabolical smile. "Shut the door," he said. "This demands total secrecy."

Oscar shut the door.

12

Two days later, Donald showed up at Oscar's place with a big clear plastic bowl of red Jell-O and a brown paper bag full of something that smelled very much like stale fish.

"That was a close one!" Donald said, out of breath. "Norval came running through the lobby just as I got in the elevator. If he'd seen me with this stuff, we would have had to change all our plans."

He handed Oscar the bag. The fishy odor got stronger. "Pee-yew! What's in here, anyway?"

"Fresh monsters!" said Donald.

Oscar made a face and stuck his nose into the bag. "Yecch!" he said. "What is this stuff?"

59

Donald just smiled. "Your parents aren't at home, are they?"

Oscar shook his head.

"Good. Let's get started. We need time to do this right." And they headed for Oscar's bedroom.

While Oscar cleared all the junk from the top of his desk, Donald took a knife and fork from the bag. "Did you make the signs?" he asked.

"They're under the bed," Oscar said.

Donald stooped down, slipped them out, and had a look. "Pretty good," he said. "Your parents didn't see these, did they?"

"Of course not," Oscar said. "Boy, I've never seen anybody so worried about keeping a secret."

"Oscar, I explained this to you before," said Donald in exasperation. "This is the biggest secret that ever existed. If either one of us makes the slightest little slip, then our whole plan is ruined. We have to be on our guard at all times. Otherwise somebody is sure to figure out what's going on. It's just lucky for us nobody recognized me the other day when you put me in the middle of that monster movie."

"They all thought you were attacking South Dakota," said Oscar. "And I know all about how secret this is."

"Well, just don't forget it. Otherwise, everything will get all messed up."

"You worry too much," said Oscar.

"We'll see," said Donald.

He set the clear plastic bowl on the desk beneath

60

the lamp. Then he picked up the bag and emptied it into the bowl. Out flopped three of the ugliest creatures Oscar had ever seen.

"What are those repulsive things, anyhow?" Oscar asked.

"Two squid and one octopus, obviously."

"Where'd you ever find them?"

"The fish market, of course."

"You mean people actually *eat* that stuff?"

"Sure. I've had them myself once or twice. Once they're dead, they don't bite back."

Oscar made another face and took a closer look at them as they lay on top of the Jell-O. "They don't move, either," he pointed out. "Who's afraid of a dead monster?"

"Don't worry about that," Donald said. "Go get a little bowl or something."

"You're not going to make a mess in here, are you? I don't think my mom would like it if you got Jell-O and squid all over the place."

Donald gave him an exasperated look. "Just go get the bowl."

Oscar went into the kitchen and came back with a cereal bowl. Donald went to work. First he put the monsters back in the bag. Then he chopped out a sort of lunar landscape in the Jell-O. He hacked the surface into strange-looking craters and spooned the extra Jell-O into the cereal bowl. Finally he put the squid and the octopus back into the Jell-O and covered them with what he had taken out. "Done!" he said.

To Oscar, it looked something like a dessert called "pineapple delight" that his mother used to make for summer picnics—only this was red and had squid and octopus in it instead of pineapple and didn't look all that delightful. Or scary, either. "How is that going to fool anybody?" Oscar wanted to know.

"Just wait," said Donald. "I'll set up the lights. You get the camera ready."

Donald turned off the overhead light and turned on Oscar's gooseneck desk lamp. Then he twisted the lamp around until it lit up the Jell-O from below, almost as if it were glowing. Oscar brought the camera.

"Ready?" Donald asked.

Oscar nodded. "What should I do?"

"Just move in there real close and see what you see."

"I see a bowl of cherry Jell-O with two squid and one octopus in it."

Donald poked the side of the bowl. "Now what do you see?"

"I see a bowl of cherry Jell-O with two squid and one octopus in it, only now the bowl is shaking a little."

"Come on, Osc! Use your imagination!"

"I *am* using my imagination. But if we're going to fool people, we can't say 'Okay, people, use your imagination!' We either fool them or we don't. And this wouldn't fool Norval's dog."

"Can you see the edge of the bowl?"

"Of course I can see the edge of the bowl."

"Then move in closer. That's probably what's spoiling the illusion."

Oscar moved in closer. Donald was right. Once you couldn't see the edge of the bowl, the picture did look kind of spooky.

Donald jiggled the bowl again. "How is it now?"

"Pretty good," Oscar said. "But there's still something phony about it."

"Let me look," said Donald. "You jiggle the bowl awhile."

They traded places.

"Don't jiggle so hard, Osc," Donald commanded.

"If it shakes too much, it really does look like a bowl of red Jell-O."

"I told you," said Oscar, easing up on his jiggles.

"Yeah, there, that's better. You just need a sort of quiver, just enough to make it look like the stuff is moving from the inside. There! That's pretty good!"

"Pretty good isn't going to fool people," Oscar reminded him.

"Then slow it down even more."

Oscar did.

"Great! Don't stop! You've got it!" Donald cried. "Quick! How do I turn on the camera?"

"Press the button marked RECORD, of course. It's on the back."

"You sure this thing won't send out any pictures while we're doing this?"

"Positive," Oscar said, beginning to get tired of being the chief Jell-O jiggler. "It only sends pictures to other places when you play tapes back through that viewfinder in the camera."

"Okay, we're on," Donald said. "Keep it nice and slow."

"Hey, we're not supposed to be talking," Oscar said.

"Huh?"

"The sound's on. That little microphone on the top picks up everything we say."

Donald put down the camera with a disgusted look. "Why didn't you tell me?"

"I was too busy jiggling," Oscar answered. "Besides, I thought I was going to be the cameraman."

They tried again. And again. And again. First they forgot to have Oscar's special message boards handy so they could shoot them right after the creepy bowl of Jell-O. Then they forgot to make the right noises. Then the Jell-O started melting. Actually, that turned out not to be a problem, because it made everything look even slimier than ever. The real problem was that the squid and the octopus were beginning to stink.

On the twenty-third try, Donald accidentally bumped the lamp. On the twenty-fourth try, everything seemed to go all right. "This time I bet it'll work," Donald said hopefully as Oscar pressed the REWIND button on the recorder.

"It'd better," Oscar said. "My parents will be home any minute."

Oscar and Donald anxiously watched the diagonal stripes on the TV screen as the tape rewound to the starting point. Then they watched the weird program they had just taped.

Donald looked at Oscar. "What do you think?"

Oscar shrugged and smiled. "It's definitely worth a try."

Donald nodded. "Let the invasion begin!"

13

It was all planned right down to the last second. Oscar just hoped his parents wouldn't catch on. When his mother got home, she noticed the unpleasant odor in his bedroom and asked Oscar if he was having stomach trouble again. Oscar just sort of grunted. At least the evidence had gone home with Donald, who was planning to find out whether there was anything interesting you could do with squid ink.

At dinner, Oscar was so excited he could barely eat, and that made his mother wonder about his stomach again. Oscar wasn't worried about his digestion. He was worried that dinner would never end.

But at last it did. Oscar went into the bedroom to prepare for the big event. He turned on the recorder, and the machine thanked him and told him it was ready. He turned on his TV to one of the stations that carried the news. A gray-haired man in a shiny suit was attacking pizza as a menace to the city's way of life.

Oscar turned on the camera. All he had to do now was wait.

He sat through a commercial for Elbow Gleam, a new spray product that was supposed to make your elbows soft and shiny. Then he saw the anchorman and heard the words "Good evening."

It was the moment Oscar had been waiting for. He pressed the PLAY button on the camera.

On the little screen inside the camera, and on the big screen of his TV set, a huge, slimy eye and a tangle of horrible tentacles slithered in a sea of red goo. Then a message appeared on the screen. It said:

EARTHLINGS!
DO NOT TOUCH YOUR TELEVISION SET.
WE HAVE TAKEN CONTROL.

The glistening tentacles returned to the screen. In the background there were groaning noises, as though the creatures were rather angry—and getting ready to do something absolutely dreadful. As

the camera moved closer, the tentacles quivered back and forth. Then another message appeared:

WE SHALL RETURN.

Oscar pressed the STOP button, and the anchorman returned to the screen just as quickly as he had disappeared. He didn't seem the slightest bit puzzled or upset about the giant tentacles and the messages that had just appeared. In fact, he didn't even seem to have noticed them. He just made a joke about the weather and introduced a commercial for spark plugs.

Ten seconds later the telephone rang—Donald, no doubt. Oscar leaped from his bed and ran out into the hallway. But the call wasn't for him—it was for his mother.

Just his luck! His mother could talk on the phone for hours. And the suspense was driving him crazy. He was dying to know if the broadcast had worked the way he'd planned it. Donald was probably trying to phone him right now.

"Wait a second," his mother said. "Oscar, were you watching the news just now?"

"Sort of half," he said.

"Did you see anything like"—his mother laughed as she said it—"some sort of strange creatures just now? On the news?"

Oscar felt a shiver of success. It had worked!

"Mostly I was doing my homework," he said as if he couldn't've cared less. "I wasn't really paying attention."

Ten minutes later, his mother got off the phone. Then Donald called. "So far so good," he said. "Go look out your window."

Oscar went to his bedroom window and looked out. He didn't see anything particularly unusual. "What's so special?" he asked.

"You mean you don't see people running around in the street as though they're afraid of being taken over by alien invaders?"

Oscar leaned over and looked down into the street to make sure. "No," he said. "Not even one."

"Me neither," Donald replied with a laugh. "Just wait."

14

"*INVADERS FROM OTHER PLANETS?* News at eleven!"

Oscar wasn't allowed to stay up that late. But he didn't have to watch the eleven o'clock news to know that an awful lot of people had been fooled by the bowl of Jell-O and the Prechtwinkle Video Camera.

For his one hour of television, Oscar decided to watch a show about record-breaking human achievements. He wanted to see the man who had built a ship entirely out of leftover corncobs and sailed it across the world's biggest frog farm. But just as the ship appeared on the screen, a news bulletin broke in. Reporters were asking residents of the Forest Glade section about the mysterious messages that had appeared on their TV screens at around six o'clock. Everybody had an opinion, but nobody seemed to know much.

There was no doubt about it. The first part of the plan had worked. Oscar went to bed dreaming happy dreams of giant squidlike creatures climbing up the tallest buildings in town and snaking out their tentacles to catch airplanes and blimps.

When he woke up the next morning, he ran

straight to the door to get the newspaper. It didn't take him long to find the story he was looking for. It was right on the front page.

TELEVISION MYSTERY!
WEIRD MESSAGES INTERRUPT
EVENING NEWS
MEANING? EXPERTS DISAGREE

Residents of the Forest Glade section of the city were shocked tonight as mysterious messages and unusual beings appeared on television sets throughout the neighborhood at approximately 6 P.M. The creatures resembled underwater animals trapped in a sticky red substance and claimed in written messages that they had taken over the airwaves.

The unusual messages appeared on all channels throughout most of the neighborhood. "It was like some kind of weird beast like I never saw before," said housewife Arlene Mervis. "They were howling and moaning the way my two kids do when they're hungry."

"They looked just like squid and octopus to me," said Giuseppe Tartini of Joe's Fish Market on 43rd Avenue. "By the way, I got 'em on special all this week—the squids, not whatever these things from outer space are."

"The weirdest thing was these messages," said Ellen Hooter of 329th Street. "They didn't say them, they only put them up on the screen for you to read, like they don't know how to talk English or some-

73

thing. Of course, that's the way it is with most animals, except for my uncle's parrot, but then he doesn't know how to write, I mean the parrot, not my uncle. These space things don't have such good handwriting, but at least they seem to know how to spell okay."

Oscar hadn't ever won prizes for penmanship, but he didn't think the writing on his message cards was all *that* bad. He read on.

Authorities are baffled as to the meaning of this strange occurrence. "Could be we have some strange beings from outer space on our hands" was the way Police Chief Otto Gorp put it. "Then again, might well be something else. Or not. We're working on it, you can bet your toenails on that."

Scientist Terence Firma of the El Mira Planetarium had a different opinion. "It is highly unlikely that alien beings would look like the ones that have been described by the eyewitnesses," said she when contacted by phone. "On the other hand, there's no reason to believe that they're *not* alien beings. To sum up: It beats me."

According to most eyewitnesses, the aliens' final message was "We'll be back." Authorities advise the public to remain calm and not panic. "There is no need," they say, "for anything other than a calm approach to the problem."

There was another story right beneath it. It said:

THE NEWS-EXPRESS POLL: ARE YOU WORRIED ABOUT ALIEN VISITORS TO YOUR TV SET?

Very	52%
Sort of	33%
I guess so	12%
Not me	10%
Huh?	8%

(Total more than 100% because some lamebrains couldn't make up their minds.)

It was front page news. It was the only thing his parents could talk about at the breakfast table. But they didn't believe it was for real.

Neither did Norval. He considered himself an expert on the subject. And he was amazed that Oscar hadn't seen the aliens. "How could you have missed them, bonehead?" he asked Oscar. "This is the biggest thing to hit the neighborhood since that time the coffee shop blew up."

"I told you," Oscar said, "I don't watch much TV."

"Well, you should've been watching last night, that's for sure. These creatures have about a million arms and legs, and they've got this creepy-looking red stuff all over them," he said, aiming a gob of spit at Oscar's left shoe.

Oscar moved his foot away just in time. "What do

you think they are?" he asked, trying hard to hold back a smirk.

"It's obvious what they are," Norval proclaimed. "They're some kind of advertising for some new movie. They probably want to scare you first and then get you to pay money to see this thing. There are no such things as monsters from other planets."

So Norval wasn't fooled yet. Donald had predicted that. It would take more than what had happened so far to put a scare in Norval.

But Mandy and most of the other kids were positive aliens were about to take over the neighborhood. Even Hughie at the Pizza Palace was sure the invaders were for real. In fact, he was working on a special Astro-pizza in their honor.

Oscar could hardly believe it. How could one bowl of Jell-O, one octopus, and two squid cause all this commotion?

"Easy," said Donald when they got together after school that afternoon. "Why, when Orson Welles did *War of the Worlds*, there wasn't even a squid or an octopus. All there was was a bunch of people talking on the radio."

He pulled some even bigger and slimier and creepier squid and octopi from his brown paper bag. "This time we'll *really* scare people. This grape Jell-O looks even worse than it tastes."

"Don't your folks get suspicious about your making all this Jell-O?"

"I just tell them I'm doing a project for school. That always does the trick."

"It amazes me what people will believe," Oscar said, as Donald artistically arranged the aliens. "You ready?"

"Shoot away," said Donald. And they both sent up horrible alien howls as Oscar turned on the camera and plunged it straight toward the intergalactic invaders.

15

Oscar watched the news that evening with a very large grin on his face. "A mystery continues to surround the appearance of unusual creatures on the television sets of the Forest Glade neighborhood," said the anchorman. "For that story, we switch you live to Roxanne Beadle, our reporter on the scene."

Oscar punched the PLAY button on the camera. A message filled the screen.

THERE IS NO MYSTERY.
WE ARE IN CONTROL.

Then came some eyes and tentacles in purple

slime and some ominous grunts and groans. Then
there was another message.

YOU HAVE NOTHING TO FEAR.
WE WISH ONLY TO REMOVE ONE CHILD
FROM YOUR PLANET FOR OBSERVATION.
THE CHILD MUST BE MALE
AND HAVE HAIR THAT IS RED.
THE CHOSEN CHILD WILL RECEIVE
A SPECIAL SIGN.
PLEASE AWAIT FURTHER INSTRUCTIONS.
THANK YOU FOR YOUR PATIENCE.
HAVE A NICE DAY!

Oscar pressed the STOP button. "Everything
seems quiet for the moment," said Roxanne Beadle,
the TV reporter. Then Oscar noticed she was standing in front of the ice-cream store right across the
street from his apartment building. "That's it for
now, Rollo," she added.

The anchorman looked as if he had swallowed a
whole octopus in one gulp. "Uh . . . well . . . Roxanne, can you hear me?"

The reporter held her hand over her ear so she
could hear better. "Yes, Rollo?"

"Uh . . . gosh . . . something remarkable has happened, Roxanne," said the bewildered anchorman.
"A new message from these . . . uh . . . well, I guess
we don't know what they are, do we? Anyhow, they

appeared on the screen and interrupted your report."

The reporter looked around as though a giant squid might crawl up her panty hose any second. "Uh-oh," she said.

"Do you have any further news to report?"

"Well, uh . . . gee . . ." she stammered.

"They're here! They've landed!" shouted a familiar voice.

The reporter looked up, and the camera tilted up to Oscar's building. An old woman in a flowered dress was out on her fire escape, hollering frantically. "Right in my own neighborhood! Help!" cried Mrs. Seltzer.

"We'll check right into this, Rollo," said Roxanne Beadle. "And we'll return with a full report later in the broadcast."

The anchorman looked very serious indeed. He said that this was the most remarkable story he had covered in a lifetime of reporting the news. He said that no one should think of touching the dial. He said he would be right back with full coverage after "this." "This" turned out to be a commercial for bubble-gum shampoo.

The phone rang. It was Donald. His building had a special television channel that showed you what was going on in the lobby. What was going on right now was that people were standing around wondering when the monsters would strike. One woman was sure she saw a big squid peeking out of the sofa, and she made the doorman take all the cushions off to check.

"Don't forget to put Plan B into action," Donald said.

"Quit worrying! I'm on my way," said Oscar, and hung up. Sometimes Donald thought he was the only person on the planet who could do things right.

Oscar went to his closet and took out a plastic bag that had a distinctly fishy aroma. Then he went to the kitchen and picked up the bag of trash from the garbage bin.

"Where are you going?" his mother inquired.

"Just taking out the garbage," he said.

"Well, this is a first! Offering to take out the garbage without my even asking!"

Oscar grinned sheepishly.

"Couldn't be you want to go outside and see if you can find any monsters, could it?" asked his father.

"Huh?" Oscar said as innocently as he could.

"They broke into our favorite Beethoven string quartet with a special radio bulletin," his mother replied. "It seems there may be some sort of alien beings loose in the neighborhood, and they're planning to snatch kids away."

"Personally, we don't really believe it ourselves," his father said—Oscar felt quietly proud that his parents hadn't been fooled—"but you can never be too careful."

"So we'd prefer it if you didn't take the garbage out tonight," said his mother.

Oscar had to get out of the apartment. Otherwise, Plan B would be in danger. "I'm not scared of any old monsters," said he. "I don't believe in them either."

"The question isn't whether you believe in them," said Mr. Noodleman. "It's whether they believe in you. We want you to stay in the apartment this evening. Just to be safe."

Oscar had never felt so frustrated in his life. He tried again. "I saw the latest message on my TV. They said they were only interested in redheaded kids."

"Oh," said his mother. "That's different."

"Well, we can't live our lives in fear," said Oscar's father. "Fine. Be thankful you're not redheaded. Take out the garbage. Enjoy it."

Oscar's mother looked thoughtful. "That awful Norval friend of yours has the reddest hair I've ever seen. I wonder what he thinks of all this."

Oscar didn't answer. He just held the garbage tight and slunk out the door.

First he went to the garbage chute. He made very sure to dump only the trash bag, not the fishy one he was holding in his other hand. Then he got on the elevator and rode it up two flights. He hoped he wouldn't meet anybody on the way. The bag smelled fishier than ever, and he didn't want anyone to suspect what he was up to.

Oscar grinned from ear to ear as he thought about what was happening. Boy, would he ever get Norval this time! This would be the biggest surprise of Norval's entire life!

Oscar bravely stuck his nose into the bag and looked inside to make sure nothing was missing. Then the elevator door opened. Without looking up, Oscar stepped out—and ran smack into Norval!

16

A look of panic replaced Oscar's grin. For a red-headed kid who might be carried off at any moment by a giant squid, Norval did not look the least bit frightened.

First he poked the elevator button marked LOBBY. Then he poked Oscar in the belly button. "What are you doing up here?" he demanded.

There was absolutely no reason for Oscar to be on the fifth floor unless he was going to visit Norval. And there was even less reason for him to be on the fifth floor with a fishy-smelling paper bag in his hands. Oscar pressed the 3 button to stall for time.

"Well?" Norval said, giving Oscar another poke for punctuation.

"I must've pressed the wrong button by mistake," Oscar said, backing away. "The elevator must've gone up instead of down."

"What's in the bag?"

"Uh . . . g-garbage," Oscar stammered.

"Since when do you take your garbage with you on the elevator?"

"Gee! I guess I goofed about that, too!" Oscar said sheepishly.

"You'd better throw it out fast," Norval said. "It really stinks."

"You're telling me!"

"I bet I know why you're all upset," Norval sneered. "You're probably all scared on account of those invaders from another planet."

Oscar did his best to pretend. "Aren't *you*?"

"Ha! That's a laugh! If they want redheaded kids, I'd like to see 'em come get *me*. Just let 'em try! I'll show those monsters a thing or two!"

You just might, Oscar thought to himself.

"Besides, I still say it's all a big joke. It's probably just advertising for a movie called something like *The Octopus That Ate Redheaded Kids* or something. You'll see."

The elevator stopped at the third floor. Oscar stepped out. "Where are you going?" Norval demanded.

"To throw this garbage away before I forget."

"You want me to hold the elevator for you?"

The last thing in the world Oscar wanted was for Norval to hold the elevator. If that happened, Oscar would have to hide his bag near the garbage chute and hope nobody threw it in before he had a chance to come back and pick it up later. What he really wanted was for Norval to disappear.

"Well, come on," said Norval. "Do you want me to hold the elevator or don't you?"

Oscar had a brainstorm. "Yeah," he replied. "I'm in kind of a hurry. *Please* hold it for me. I'll only be a second. Just hang on. Don't leave."

"Sure," said Norval.

Oscar got off the elevator and walked around the corner. "So long, stupid!" Norval shouted.

Oscar heard the elevator doors close. The brainstorm had worked. Now all he had to do was press the button and wait for the elevator again.

When it came back up, nobody was inside. Oscar breathed a sigh of relief as he rode to the fifth floor.

Before he stepped out, he made sure nobody was looking. Then he walked down the hallway, stopped in front of Norval's door, and stooped down. He reached into his bag. He took out two slimy, repulsive octopi and three sickening squid, and deposited them right in the middle of Norval's welcome mat.

Back in his own apartment, he phoned Donald. "Mission accomplished," said he.

"Excellent," said Donald. "We can't fail."

17

The next morning, Norval was not at school. In fact, the only redheaded guy in Oscar's class who showed up was a kid named Peter. He said his parents weren't worried about the giant squid taking him away. They said if it happened, it happened, and it would be an excellent learning experience, and if he survived, he would be famous and could make a lot of money going on TV and talking about his adventures in space.

The alien invaders were the only thing anybody talked about in school that day. In fact, they were the only thing anybody talked about in the whole city that day. The newspapers had headlines like

ALIENS RETURN!
SQUID MAKE CITY SQUIRM

and

SLIME TIME IN PRIME TIME
OOZE NEWS GIVES REDHEADS BLUES

The police determined that the strange broad-casts definitely had nothing to do with publicity for any movies, but otherwise the authorities were stumped. The Army Reserves were mobilized just in case the aliens got nasty.

Dozens of reporters arrived in the neighborhood from all over the world. Some of them even turned up at Oscar's school to interview the kids about how they felt. Norval was right about one thing: This was the biggest event that had ever taken place in the neighborhood of Forest Glade.

"Well, what did I tell you?" Donald said when he and Oscar got together after school.

Oscar shook his head. "I still can hardly believe this," he admitted. "But what now?"

"Now," said Donald. "It's time for a break."

"A break?"

"Sure. Everybody for miles around is expecting another message tonight at six. Well, this time, there won't be a message. That'll make the whole thing all the more mysterious and frustrating."

Oscar had to admire Donald's planning. "How do you figure all this stuff out?"

"When you've seen as many monster movies as I have, there's nothing to it. This is just like a story. Except it's real."

It was so real that even Oscar's parents wanted to watch the news on TV that night. He had to bring his set into the living room so everyone could watch during dinner, something his parents normally had a strict rule against.

According to the news, the whole city was standing by to see what would happen next. Scientists were standing by, ready to record the latest message so that they could check to see what sort of creatures these invaders really were and decide whether the whole thing was merely some sort of elaborate hoax. Reporters were standing by in television stores, department stores, barrooms, and living rooms—anywhere there was a TV set—to await the latest message. Even innocent bystanders were standing by.

Oscar sort of felt sorry for them. Six o'clock came and went, and there was no sign of an alien. Not even a little one.

"We can only hope that the the trying ordeal of the Forest Glade community is over," said the anchorman in his most serious tones. "But the neighborhood children have had a scare they may never forget."

Suddenly Oscar saw that redheaded kid Peter on the screen. He was being interviewed, saying he wasn't really scared or anything. Then Oscar popped up and told the reporter he was glad he wasn't redheaded. It was the tape from one of the

90

interviews at school that afternoon. Oscar's parents said he looked good on TV, and Oscar didn't think he looked so bad himself.

By the time the news ended, there still had been no new message. All the bystanders seemed baffled.

Norval phoned a few minutes later.

"Why weren't you in school today?" Oscar asked.

"I had a cold," Norval said.

"You sound fine to me."

"Yeah, well, I'm feeling much better now."

I'll bet, Oscar thought.

"Did we have any homework?" Norval asked.

"A little," Oscar answered. "Mrs. Larson said you didn't have to do it if you were redheaded. A lot of redheaded guys didn't go to school today."

"Maybe this cold is going around," Norval said.

Sure is, thought Oscar. "Hey, I wonder if anybody got that message from the aliens yet."

"Yeah," Norval mumbled.

"How do *you* know?"

Norval hemmed and hawed. "Well, uh, I just meant somebody must've got the message, that's all. It just makes sense, right?"

"I thought you thought this was all a big gag."

"Now I'm not so sure."

"Are you going to be in school tomorrow?"

"I, uh . . . I don't know. It depends on my cold."

"Well, there weren't any aliens on TV tonight. Maybe they changed their minds about taking that redheaded kid to their planet or whatever horrible thing it is they want to do with him."

"Yeah. Maybe."

"If somebody did get that message, I guess we'd know it soon enough. The poor kid would probably be spooked out of his mind."

"You never know," said Norval.

Oscar went into his bedroom and bounced around on the mattress. He was going to get back at Norval all right, he thought gleefully. He was going to get back and more. Tomorrow would be a day that Norval would never forget as long as he lived.

Oscar felt giddy as he sat down at his desk and started his homework. The plan was going better than he could have dreamed. "Aliens disappear!" cried the TV from the living room. "News at eleven!"

Oscar shut his door. He didn't need to stay up till eleven to know that nobody would discover any more aliens that night. He jumped onto his bed and bounced up and down on the mattress some more.

Suddenly he felt something grab his ankle. The something felt rather cool and slimy.

He looked toward the foot of the bed. A huge eye looked back at him. And two enormous tentacles were wrapping themselves around each of his legs.

"Uh-oh," said Oscar Noodleman.

18

Whatever it was at the foot of the bed had the strongest tentacles Oscar had ever felt. And the biggest. Holding on tight, they flung Oscar way up in the air and then slammed him back down on the bed. Oscar was glad he had a nice bouncy mattress. But at the moment, that was the only thing he had to be glad about.

"Are you making fun of us, Mr. Noodleman?" asked a deep gurgly voice that sounded as though it came from the very bottom of the ocean.

"N-n-n-n-no," Oscar stammered.

"Are you sure?" asked that same deep voice.

"Y-y-y-y-yes!" Oscar stuttered.

The tentacles eased their grip a little. "Then what *are* you trying to do?"

"Huh?"

The tentacles squeezed harder. "You know what I mean."

"I don't!" Oscar cried. "Honest!"

The tentacles flung Oscar up and down again. It was very embarrassing. It also hurt a little. "Tell the truth. Why are you sending unauthorized messages and pretending they come from us?"

"Who are you?" Oscar asked.

"I'll ask the questions, thank you," said the huge shapeless thing at the foot of the bed. "Now, are you

or are you not the person who is responsible for sending those phony messages that are scaring everybody in the neighborhood?"

"Not all by myself," Oscar squeaked.

"So you admit it," said the giant whatsit. "Now, what are you going to do about it?"

Oscar decided to be brave. He had to be smarter than a squid (or whatever it was), no matter how big the squid (or whatever it was) might be. "Nothing," he said firmly.

An instant later he felt himself being hoisted in the air and flung down onto the bed again. It was kind of like being a human whip. He decided to try a different approach.

"Can I ask a question?"

"Oh, I suppose," the creature muttered. "Just don't get uppity."

"Well, are you really from outer space or what?"

"Outer space? Where'd you ever get that idea?"

"I don't know."

"Boy, are you ever confused. I'm from inner space—Davy Jones's locker. The briny deep. The world beneath the waves."

Oscar took two deep breaths. There was definitely a salty seaside tang in the air. "How did you get here, then?"

"You certainly ask silly questions. I swam, of course. And believe me, it's no fun swimming in the sewer system, especially where it gets all narrow in your bathtub. I nearly lost a tentacle."

"So why did you bother?"

The tentacles gripped tighter around Oscar's leg, and he braced himself for another ride to the ceiling and back. But this time the creature didn't toss him up. In fact, it almost sounded sad. "Did you ever live in the ocean?"

Oscar shook his head.

"No, I don't suppose you did. Well, it's not easy anymore, I can tell you that. For thousands of years we lived in peace—except, of course, when bigger creatures decided to eat us—but now look what's happened. People everywhere! People take our relatives away in huge nets. People dive down to spy on us in funny rubber suits. People hit us on the head with their surfboards. People dump their garbage in our homes. People play their awful radios at the beach. How would you like it if I took your

mother away in a net, hit you on the head with a surfboard, dumped garbage in your bed, and played the Top 40 underwater hits at ear-blasting volume over and over again?"

"Not much," Oscar said sympathetically.

"Well, this television business of yours is the last straw. We keep hearing about it on the radio news between those horrible songs. The last thing we want to do is take redheaded kids away with us to study. First of all, they'd probably drown. Second of all, if they didn't drown, they'd probably play their awful music. And third of all, we just want to live our wet, quiet lives."

"I think this is all a big misunderstanding," Oscar said. And he tried to explain what he and Donald had been doing.

Unfortunately, the creature did not entirely understand it. "Aliens from outer space! How absurd! I do not believe any species on the face of the earth —no, not even humans—could be so stupid as to swallow these idiotic stories of yours."

"That's what I thought," said Oscar. "We're both wrong."

"And even if I did believe it, I certainly could never get my relatives to understand. They want these broadcasts stopped pronto. That's why I'm here."

"But we didn't send any messages tonight," Oscar pointed out.

"Hmmmm," said the creature thoughtfully. "Then you won't do it anymore?"

"Just once. After that, we'll stop."

The tentacles tightened uncomfortably again. "Not good enough, Mr. Noodleman."

"Are you going to toss me up and down again?" Oscar asked.

"Do you want me to?"

"Not really."

"Well, then, be sensible. Just say you won't do any more of those stupid TV messages."

"Not even just one?" Oscar asked.

"Not even half of one."

"I don't know. . . ." said Oscar.

The tentacles gripped tighter. Oscar's ankles felt extremely sore.

"Okay," he said.

"Promise?"

"Sure."

"Say it."

"I promise."

"I promise what?"

Whatever this creature was, it was getting to be almost as obnoxious as Norval. Oscar decided to humor it. "I promise I won't send out any more TV messages like the ones I did before."

"Cross your heart and hope to die."

"Aw, come on," Oscar said irritably. "Enough already."

"Well, all right, I guess," said the beast. "But I'm warning you. If you don't keep your promise, you'll be in big trouble."

A flash of silver-blue light filled the room. A clap of thunder made Oscar sit up on his bed with a start. He looked around the room.

There was no creature anywhere. There was a faint salty tang in the air—probably left over from yesterday's bag of seafood. Oscar felt as though he had just woken up from a nightmare. In fact, he was sure of it.

19

All the redheaded guys were back at school the next day. All but Norval.

Every time Oscar thought about what he was going to do to that rotten kid, a big smile would break out on his face. But then he'd start thinking about his promise to the giant sea creature, and his smile would vanish.

He knew it was ridiculous. If somebody in a dream promises to give you a million dollars, you can't go out and spend it next morning when you wake up. Oscar thought it should work both ways. He shouldn't have to keep a promise in real life just because he made one in a dream.

He decided to check with Donald about it just to

be safe. He knew Donald would be very interested in hearing about the monster in the dream. Besides, if Oscar broke his promise, Donald might get in trouble, too.

"Nothing to worry about," Donald assured him. "Dream-promises don't count."

"If it was a dream."

"It had to be. You know I'm an expert on monsters. First, monsters do not just show up and disappear like that, except in dreams and the very crummiest movies. Second, monsters don't ask people to make promises. They either kill you or they don't."

"I sure hope you're right," Oscar said. "That thing was big enough to eat us."

"Don't worry. Squid and octopi don't eat humans. People would give them a really terrible stomachache. Now come on. We've got to get this stuff on tape before your parents come home."

Oscar and Donald were old hands at taping by now. It went faster than ever. When they played the tape back, it looked absolutely perfect. Oscar grinned at Donald. Donald grinned at Oscar. It was going to be the greatest moment in television history.

There was one minor problem. Oscar's parents still had his television set out in the living room. They felt it was their duty as parents to watch the evening news and make sure there were no aliens from space running around the neighborhood and removing children for observation. They said he should watch with them, but he told them he had a lot of homework to catch up on. He didn't dare let them in on the secret, so he stayed in the bedroom and listened to the news through the open door.

Through the door, Oscar could hear the anchorman reporting—or was it complaining?—that the mysterious aliens hadn't been heard from in two days. The authorities had no new information.

Then Oscar pressed the PLAY button on his camera, and the mammoth octopi filled the screens—in the camera and out in the living room and all through the neighborhood—for their final performance. This time they were in a bright green slime, and they sounded angrier than ever.

Then lettering appeared:

We have selected
NORVAL MOLARSKY
of
157890 333rd Street, Apartment 5D.

If he is in front of his building
at exactly 6:30 this evening,
he will not be harmed.
If he does not show up . . .
earthlings, you have been warned.

"Oscar!" shouted his parents. He pressed the OFF button and calmly went into the living room.

"You are never going to believe this," said his mother. On the screen, the newscaster urged his

102

viewers to stay tuned for special coverage of a historic event, live from Forest Glade.

"What am I not going to believe?" Oscar asked innocently.

"They chose their victim."

Oscar shrugged. "They said they were going to."

"But now they've said who it is," said his father.

"Who?"

"Norval."

Oscar decided he'd have more fun playing dumb. "Which Norval?"

"Which Norval do you think?" His mother pointed to the TV set.

Oscar watched. On the screen was the latest message from the aliens, only with the letters **TAPE: RECORDED MOMENTS AGO** superimposed over it. "Wow!" Oscar shouted. "Right here on 333rd Street! I'll be able to tape the whole thing with my camera!"

"You are not leaving this apartment, young man," said Mr. Noodleman. "If there are aliens out there, we're certainly not going to let them snatch you."

"But they said they only want Norval. I want to see what's going on."

"You can watch on television, or you can watch from your window. That's final."

"Aw, but Mom . . ."

"Final," his father repeated.

Oscar knew there was no use trying to argue. Even though he'd planned to tape the arrival of the aliens from downstairs, he knew he'd just have to make do.

The television station covered the story from every possible angle. The political correspondent discussed how the invaders might affect the upcoming primary election. The science specialist asked psychologists whether it was better to smile or to frown at alien beings. The medical expert explained that aliens could be hazardous to your health. The sports expert claimed fewer people were going to stadiums for fear they might be snatched up by a giant octopus. The fashion correspondent reported a new fad: hats with tentacles. And the weatherman forecast that there was a ten percent chance it might rain squid ink.

Sirens began blaring outside. Oscar ran to his bedroom window. Everywhere he looked—in the street below, on balconies and fire escapes across the way, even up on the light poles—crowds were beginning to gather. Police cars and fire trucks and army jeeps were closing off the area. Oscar saw camera vans from Channels 2, 4, 6, 8, 11, 34, 62, H, R, and 193. But there was no sign of Norval.

Oscar picked up his camera. He leaned way out of the window and looked through the viewfinder. No Norval. The time-and-temperature clock outside the bank ticked away. 6:25. 72f. 22c. 6:26. 70f. 2 c. (The 1 had been broken for the last five years.) 6:27. Still no Norval. But Oscar spotted Donald on his balcony across the street.

Then Oscar noticed a bright orange head of hair

right below him. It kept moving forward in jerks and twitching anxiously from side to side. Then a bunch of policemen came toward it. It froze. There was no doubt about it. Norval Molarsky was scared right down to his scalp.

6:28. 70f. 2 c. 6:29. The crowd became so quiet the only sounds Oscar could hear were chittering pigeons, along with the loud whispers of reporters explaining that this was the most historic occasion they could remember.

Suddenly a roar whooshed down from the sky, a roar so deafening it seemed unearthly. The crowd looked up. It was the nonstop for Chicago, the plane that passed overhead every night at exactly 6:30 with such a commotion that the whole neighborhood had gotten up a petition about it. As the noise died down, there was a disappointed sigh from the crowd. Then a hush fell over the street again.

Then from out of nowhere, something plummeted to the middle of the street with an overwhelming *SQUISH!* Oscar used the camera to zoom in on it. It looked suspiciously like four squid and three octopi in a broken plastic bag of lemon Jell-O.

A dozen policemen quickly surrounded it. Oscar zoomed in for a close-up of Norval quaking in his shoes. The police drew their guns. The chief tiptoed toward the mess.

Neither the Jell-O nor the creatures made any suspicious moves. The chief motioned with his gun for Norval to come over.

Norval shook his head and drew back.

"We'll protect you," said the chief.

Norval just stood there. He was quivering even more than the Jell-O.

"Hey, what's this?" one of the policemen said, noticing what looked like a piece of paper beneath one of the squid.

"Maybe it's a message," said another.

And a third policeman hurried over with long

tongs so that he could pick up the message without having to touch the squid or the slime. He handed the message delicately to a policeman with rubber gloves on his hands and a serious look on his face. That policeman held it under the nose of the chief, who had an even more serious look. Oscar zoomed in as the chief read the message out loud.

The cosmic forces have spared you, said the note. *Consider yourself fortunate. With his treachery, meanness, and offensiveness, Norval Molarsky mortally offended us and a lot of humans besides. We hope—for his sake and the sake of the planet—that this will teach him a lesson he will never forget.*

Oscar quickly swept the camera over to catch Norval's face. It lit up the little viewfinder of the camera with a bright beet red.

"What did you do to offend these alien beings, sonny?" the police chief asked.

"I—I can't think of a thing," Norval stammered. "Honest!"

"He's a rotten kid," somebody shouted from the crowd.

"He's mean and nasty!" cried somebody else.

"He plays tricks!"

"He's obnoxious!"

Norval looked as though he were actually shrinking.

"He could have offended these here aliens without even trying!" shouted still another person.

"Hear, hear!"

"He's the worst kid in the whole neighborhood!"

Norval looked as though he could fit down the bathtub drain.

The police chief stared him in the eye. "Well, sonny," he said sternly, "all I can say is, if we get any more aliens coming around these parts, you'll be in a real pickle, you can bet your grandma on that. If I were you, I'd be on my best behavior for a good little while."

Norval looked as though he wished he were anyplace else in the world.

The chief turned around. "Okay, men, scoop up

those squid and Jell-O, or whatever the heck they are! We have to take them down to the lab and find out!"

Reporters crowded around Norval and asked him a million stupid questions about how he felt. But before he could open his mouth to answer, Norval's father stormed up and grabbed his son by the arm. "That's enough questions!" Mr. Molarsky shouted, dragging Norval away. "You know what I told you I'd do if you kept on doing things that made people angry! But did you listen? Not you! You even made squids and octopuses mad!"

As they walked toward the building, Oscar leaned way out the window and got an excellent shot of a tear running down Norval's cheek. Norval looked so totally humiliated, Oscar almost felt sorry for him.

But an instant later Oscar suddenly felt something give his camera a hard push. He tried to hang on to it, but he felt himself falling out the window. As he tumbled out, he grabbed the window frame—just in time to keep from falling three stories to the street!

The camera wasn't so lucky. It slipped from his grasp, dropped to the sidewalk, and crashed with a sickening tinkle.

Oscar rushed out of the bedroom in a hurry to get downstairs. But as he passed the bathroom, he thought he saw a huge dark tentacle slither down the bathtub drain. He also thought he heard a voice that sounded as though it came from underwater say "I warned you. . . ."

20

Did he really see it? Did he really hear it? There was no time to wonder. He had to find out what had happened to his camera—the only one like it in the entire world!

He raced down the hallway and unlocked the door. "Hey! Where do you think you're going?" his mother called from the living room.

"I dropped my camera out the window!" he shouted. "I'll be right back!" He hurried out the door and ran to the elevator.

He pressed the button. The doors opened right away. And there, standing right in front of him, was Norval, looking as forlorn as a dead squid—and his father, as stern as a space warrior.

"Down?" Oscar asked.

"Up!" snorted Mr. Molarsky. The door slid closed.

Oscar kept a careful watch behind him. So far, he hadn't seen any more tentacles, but he wasn't going to let his guard down.

Finally the elevator came back. Oscar rode downstairs and hurried out through the lobby to see if his camera was still all right.

It wasn't. A large woman wearing what looked like a small tent had picked up the part of it that was still

111

in one piece. The rest was a bunch of fragments of glass and metal scattered all around.

"Excuse me," Oscar said politely. "That's my camera."

"Then you're the person I'm going to sue!" the woman cried. "That thing came within a foot of hitting my head! You TV reporters are all alike!"

Donald pushed through the crowd to where Oscar was standing. "He's not a reporter, ma'am," Donald told the woman in his politest tones. "He's just a kid. It was an accident."

"Humph," the woman said. "I suppose if I sue him, I won't get a cent."

"Nope," said Donald sympathetically.

"Just my luck!" she complained. "A camera nearly falls on my head, and it turns out to belong to somebody who doesn't have any money." Shaking her head, she handed the battered hunk of camera over to Oscar.

Oscar looked it over and sighed. "Boy! There's no chance this will work now."

"Well, it was fun while it lasted," said Donald.

"Yeah," Oscar agreed.

"You know, I almost felt sorry for Norval for a minute there."

"Yeah," Oscar admitted as he went around picking up various pieces of the camera. "Me, too."

"But only almost!" they both said at the same time.

"Well, see you tomorrow!" Donald said. "Watch out for giant squid."

A shiver ran down Oscar's spine. He hoped there

wouldn't be any tentacled creatures upstairs when he got back. He picked up all the chunks of his camera that he could find. A little kid handed him a hunk of the lens barrel. "I'm sure glad *I* didn't do that," said the kid.

Oscar trudged back inside and took the elevator up to his apartment. "Is the camera all right?" his mother called as he came in.

"Not exactly," Oscar called back, hoping he wouldn't find any tentacles reaching out for him.

"Do you think you can fix it?"

"I'll try," he said.

Oscar dug up the notebook that came with the camera. On the inside cover it said:

Important! The Model X-One is the first video camera ever created by the world renowned inventor, Dr. Peter Prechtwinkle. It is one of a kind, and it is still experimental. This means it may not always work exactly as expected or intended.

Do not be alarmed if the camera malfunctions. This is absolutely normal with a brand-new product. Future models will correct such problems. Only with the help of you, the user, can we hope to improve our product. If you discover unusual difficulties not covered in our manual, please phone our toll-free hot line number. The call will not cost you a cent, and the number is open twenty-four hours a day, seven days a week, to serve you better. The number is:

(800) 555–6666

(except in Greater Secaucus, New Jersey: dial 555–7777)

113

Maybe if Oscar phoned, somebody could tell him how to fix the camera, or at least where to send the pieces. He set them on his desk, brought the phone into the bedroom, and dialed the toll-free number.

"Prechtwinkle Hot Line," said a friendly female voice. "How may we help you?"

"I, uh, need some information about the Prechtwinkle Video Camera."

"Oh, you must be Oscar Noodleman."

"How'd you guess?"

"Well, there's only one Prechtwinkle Video Camera in the entire world, and it's supposed to be checked out to an Oscar Noodleman, so unless you stole it, you must be him."

Oscar wanted to dig a deep hole and dive in. "I'm him, all right," he said in a very small, high voice.

"So what's the problem?"

Oscar stammered and stumbled and hemmed and hawed. His voice turned even smaller and higher as he said, "It accidentally fell out a window."

"How many stories up?" asked the woman, who did not sound quite as friendly as before.

"Three," Oscar said.

"How many pieces is it in?"

Oscar's voice was positively tiny now. "Lots," he said.

"One moment, please," the woman snapped.

The next thing Oscar heard was a loud click. After that he heard some strange polka music that kept repeating the words "Hey! Hey! Hold on!" over and over. Next he heard another click. And then he heard something like a snarl.

"How dare you break my one and only video camera!" the deep growling voice spluttered.

"It was an accident?" Oscar whimpered.

"Accident, my big toe!" screamed the voice. "It was carelessness, that's what it was! Do you know who this is?"

"No," Oscar squeaked.

"This is Dr. Peter Prechtwinkle. And that camera was my pride and joy! You'll pay for this—every cent!"

"How much?" Oscar dared to ask.

"Forty-nine thousand, four hundred sixty-two dollars and thirty-seven cents. Plus tax!" Dr. Prechtwinkle boomed.

Oscar felt faint. "I'm just a kid!" he cried. "I hardly have any money at all, except for maybe sixty-five dollars or so in the bank!"

"I'm sure we can work something out," Dr. Prechtwinkle said in calm, mellow tones. "Perhaps you can spend the summer working for me."

"But I've got plans for the summer," Oscar said. The last thing he wanted to do was spend his summer working for his strange cousin. "Why did you ever send me that stupid camera anyway?"

"Because you, Oscar J. Noodleman, are my very favorite cousin," said Dr. Prechtwinkle. "Or you *were*, until this happened."

"Me?" Oscar said in amazement. "You don't even know me!"

"That," said Dr. Peter Prechtwinkle, "is precisely why I used to like you so much. See you this summer!" And he hung up.

The Oscar J. Noodleman Television Network was out of business for good. But it left a lasting impression on the community. Dottie's Luncheonette around the corner began serving Alienburgers—a healthful blend of squid, octopus, and your choice

of cherry, grape or lime Jell-O on a sesame bun. Glade Stationers sold ink in bottles labeled "Alien

Juice." Donald enjoyed replaying his tapes of the monsters on his giant ten-foot TV screen.

As for Oscar, he kept expecting huge tentacles to invade his dreams or maybe even his real life. But the only monster he had to deal with was Dr. Peter Prechtwinkle, who phoned every couple of days with nasty screeches about people who borrowed things and didn't take care of them. It looked as though Oscar might indeed spend the summer working for his cousin.

For some strange reason, Norval seemed to have changed a lot. He was different somehow, a lot calmer and a lot less of a bully. For about two weeks. Then he tied Oscar's shoelaces together while he wasn't looking and sent him sprawling.

As Norval roared with laughter, Oscar gazed toward the galaxies and smiled a fiendish smile.

Norval apologized to Oscar real fast.